BUBBLE BUBBLE

BY MERCER MAYER

Parents' Magazine Press/New York

Copyright © 1973 by Mercer Mayer
All rights reserved
Printed in the United States of America

Library of Congress Cataloging in Publication Data

Mayer, Mercer, 1943-
    Bubble bubble.

    SUMMARY: A little boy creates all sorts of
fantastic animals with his magic bubble maker.
    (1. Stories without words) I. Title.
PZ7.M462Bu   (E)   72-6167
ISBN 0-8193-0630-4   ISBN 0-8193-0631-2 (lib. bdg.)

For Laura, Leon and John Levin